Lerner SPORTS™

SPORTS ALL-STARS

CODY BELLINGER

Jon M. Fishman

Lerner Publications ◆ Minneapolis

Lerner Publications Company
An imprint of Lerner Publishing Group, Inc.
241 First Avenue North
Minneapolis, MN 55401 USA

For reading levels and more information, look up this title at www.lernerbooks.com.

Main body text set in Albany Std. Typeface provided by Agfa.

Photo Editor: Brianna Kaiser

Library of Congress Cataloging-in-Publication Data

Names: Fishman, Jon M., author.
Title: Cody Bellinger / Jon M. Fishman.
Description: Minneapolis : Lerner Publications, 2021. | Series: Sports all-stars (Lerner Sports) | Includes bibliographical references and index. | Audience: Ages 7–11 years | Audience: Grades 4–6 | Summary: "In his first MLB season, Cody Bellinger of the Los Angeles Dodgers was unanimously voted the National League Rookie of the Year. Sports fans will love this action-packed look at a rising baseball star"— Provided by publisher.
Identifiers: LCCN 2020028322 (print) | LCCN 2020028323 (ebook) | ISBN 9781728420547 (Library Binding) | ISBN 9781728423135 (Paperback) | ISBN 9781728420561 (eBook)
Subjects: LCSH: Bellinger, Cody, 1995—-Juvenile literature. | Outfielders (Baseball)—United States—Biography—Juvenile literature. | Baseball players—United States—Biography—Juvenile literature. | Los Angeles Dodgers (Baseball team)—History—Juvenile literature. | Rookie of the Year Award (Baseball)—History—Juvenile literature. | Most Valuable Player Award (Baseball)—History—Juvenile literature. | Major League Baseball (Organization)—History—Juvenile literature. | Baseball—United States—History—Juvenile literature.
Classification: LCC GV865.B346 F57 2021 (print) | LCC GV865.B346 (ebook) | DDC 796.357092 [B]—dc23

LC record available at https://lccn.loc.gov/2020028322
LC ebook record available at https://lccn.loc.gov/2020028323

Manufactured in the United States of America
1-49149-49297-9/28/2020

TABLE OF CONTENTS

GAME WINNER

Cody Bellinger runs around the bases after hitting a home run in Game 7 of the 2018 NLCS.

Baseball fans stood and cheered at Miller Park in Milwaukee, Wisconsin. The Los Angeles Dodgers and Milwaukee Brewers were going toe-to-toe in Game 7 of the 2018 National League Championship Series (NLCS). The winner would play the Boston Red Sox in the World Series.

FACTS AT A GLANCE

- **Date of birth:** July 13, 1995
- **Position:** first base; outfield
- **League:** Major League Baseball (MLB)
- **Professional highlights:** won the 2017 National League (NL) Rookie of the Year award; won the 2019 NL Most Valuable Player (MVP) award; played in the 2017 and 2018 World Series
- **Personal highlights:** grew up in Chandler, Arizona; played in the 2007 Little League World Series; is a member of the Chandler Sports Hall of Fame

The NLCS had been full of drama. Three of the games were decided by one run. Game 4 was tied until the 13th inning. Then outfielder Cody Bellinger's RBI won the game for Los Angeles. No one could predict what would happen in Game 7.

Milwaukee's Christian Yelich hit a home run in the first inning. The blast gave the Brewers a 1–0 lead. In the second inning, Manny Machado got on base for the Dodgers. Then Bellinger stepped to the plate.

Bellinger slams a home run.

With a count of two balls and two strikes, the Milwaukee pitcher threw the ball right where Bellinger liked it. The outfielder took a massive swing. *Crack!* The ball rocketed over the outfield wall. It landed in the stadium's second level for a huge home run.

Bellinger celebrates teammate Yasiel Puig's home run.

Bellinger ran around the bases as his teammates celebrated. The Dodgers had a one-run lead, and that was all they needed. Los Angeles won 5–1.

The Dodgers advanced to the World Series for the second straight year. Bellinger was grateful. "I know how lucky I am to be a part of it two years in a row," he said. After losing in 2017, Los Angeles was determined to win the World Series in 2018.

WORLD SERIES FAMILY

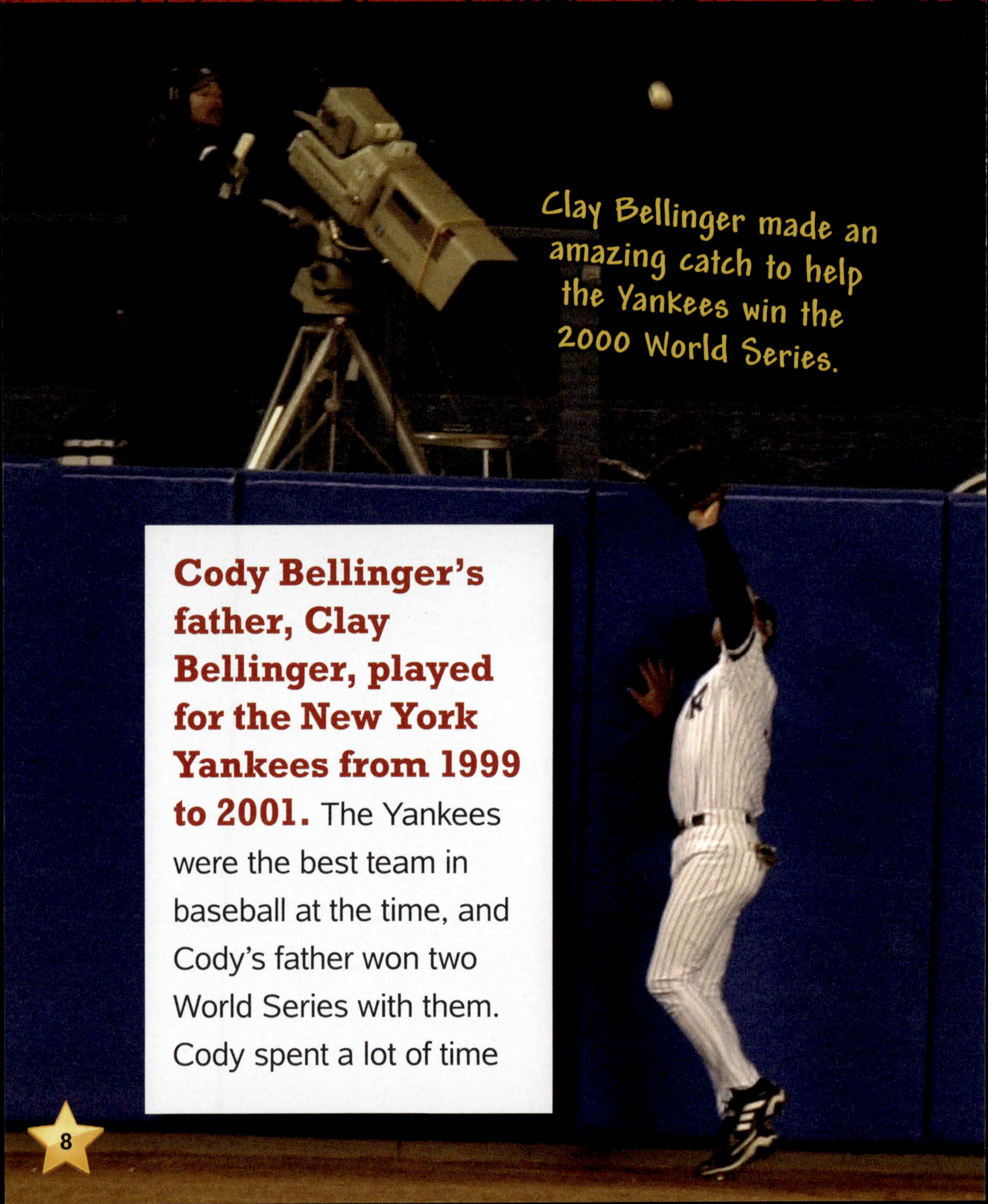

Clay Bellinger made an amazing catch to help the Yankees win the 2000 World Series.

Cody Bellinger's father, Clay Bellinger, played for the New York Yankees from 1999 to 2001. The Yankees were the best team in baseball at the time, and Cody's father won two World Series with them. Cody spent a lot of time with the team. He got an up-close look at the world's best players. When Cody started playing baseball, he fell in love with it right away.

Chandler National Little League was an all-star team of the best players from the area. Cody played first base and outfield. His father was one of the team's coaches. When Cody was 12, Chandler won game after game. They made it all the way to the 2007 Little League World Series (LLWS).

Clay (*left*) coached Cody (*right*) on the Chandler National team.

On July 13, 1995, Cody Bellinger was born in Scottsdale, Arizona. He grew up in Chandler, Arizona, with his sister, Ashli, and brother, Cole.

The LLWS takes place in Williamsport, Pennsylvania. Each year, 16 teams from around the world compete for the Little League Baseball championship. In 2007, Chandler's first game was against a team from Salisbury, Maryland.

Cody already had two hits when he came up to bat in the third inning. Chandler led 7–4. Cody blasted the third pitch, sending it to the grass beyond the outfield fence. He finished the game with four hits as Chandler won 16–6.

Young Cody at the Little League World Series in 2007

Cody (*right*) celebrates with his Chandler teammates.

After a loss and another win, Chandler fell to a team from Warner Robins, Georgia. Chandler's LLWS was over. For Cody and his teammates, playing in the LLWS was like playing MLB. Chandler's games aired on ESPN. Cody even talked about his team in an interview on the TV network.

When Cody played in the LLWS, he was 5 feet 1 (1.5 m). By 2012–2013, his senior year at Hamilton High School, he was 6 feet 3 (1.9 m). His baseball skills were incredible. He had a .429 batting average and won Hamilton's MVP award.

Bellinger warms up before a game against the Arizona League Athletics, a minor league team, in 2013.

Cody planned to attend the University of Oregon after high school. But the Dodgers chose him in the fourth round of the 2013 MLB draft. He changed his plans and headed for the minor leagues.

DOING THE LEGWORK

Bellinger at the plate in 2019

In the spring and summer, each MLB team usually plays 162 regular-season games. Some weeks, teams play every day. That doesn't leave Bellinger with much time or energy for workouts. But during the off-season, he spends a lot of time in the gym.

Bellinger (left) and teammate Justin Turner warm up before a game.

"I work on my legs a lot—that's where my power comes from," Bellinger said. "Playing every day, your legs can get tired and you have to get your strength back under you."

To strengthen his legs, Bellinger performs different kinds of squats. He also does dead lifts. Bellinger stands next to a heavy barbell. Then he bends down and lifts the barbell to his hips. He also does exercises for his upper body, especially his stomach, back, and chest.

Bellinger leaps to catch the ball and prevent a home run in 2019.

Bellinger (*right*) stretches with teammates Mookie Betts (*left*) and Justin Turner (*center*) during spring training in 2020.

Bellinger stretches his muscles after workouts. He says stretching helps him feel better the next day and helps to prevent injuries. Food is another important way that Bellinger stays healthy. He eats healthful food before and after workouts. Bellinger has meat, usually fish or chicken, with most of his meals. He also eats a lot of rice and vegetables.

To get ready for the 2019 MLB season, Bellinger worked with Dodgers hitting coaches. They noticed that Bellinger sometimes changed the way he held the bat. This meant the bat would start out in different positions when he swung, making it hard for Bellinger to be a consistent hitter.

The coaches helped Bellinger take a more relaxed position. "You are a lot better when you are calm in the [batter's] box, in the mind and the body," Bellinger said. "It's about feeling good, having confidence."

The off-season work paid off in big ways. In 2019, Bellinger set career highs with a .305 batting average, 47 home runs, and 115 RBIs. It was one of the best seasons in Dodgers history.

In 2019, Bellinger led the Los Angeles offense. He topped the team in hits, runs, home runs, RBIs, stolen bases, and several other stats.

ROLE MODEL

Bellinger signs an autograph before a game in 2018.

Bellinger's former coaches at Hamilton High School have followed his rise to baseball stardom. Current Hamilton players watch him too. "As a team, at practice, we're always talking about what he did the night before," a Hamilton pitcher said.

In the off-season, Bellinger visits Hamilton to greet the players and coaches. He has stayed connected to the area, and his hometown fans love him. In 2019, Bellinger was inducted into the Chandler Sports Hall of Fame.

Cody at Hamilton High School in 2012

Bellinger has played first base and outfield since his Little League days. In 2019, he played 36 games at first base, 25 games in center field, and 115 games in right field.

Bellinger at the Blue Diamond Gala in 2019

Bellinger spends time helping others. He visits youth centers, plays in charity golf events, and raises money to fight hunger. In 2019, he attended the fifth Blue Diamond Gala. The yearly event raises money for the Los Angeles Dodgers Foundation. Among other things, the foundation promised to build 75 youth baseball fields by 2033.

At the Blue Diamond Gala, Bellinger, his teammates, and team officials ate dinner and took part in a charity auction. Then singer Bruno Mars performed a private concert for them.

Cody Bellinger Live!

In 2018, Bellinger appeared on the TV show *Jimmy Kimmel Live!* In a fun interview, he talked about his father, his teammates, and playing for Los Angeles.

Bellinger told a funny story about a time when he and other rookies with the Dodgers dressed up as music legend Elvis Presley. He also gave the audience a laugh when he talked about riding his electric scooter to get breakfast. He said he ordered the same food every day: a banana crepe, hash browns, bacon, and two eggs.

Bellinger arrives for his appearance on *Jimmy Kimmel Live!* in 2018.

Bellinger runs to second base in a 2017 game against the Chicago Cubs.

MLB players make a lot of money. Bellinger earned almost $13 million in his first three seasons. Yet that's just a small portion of what he may make in the future. He keeps getting better and more popular. To keep him for the rest of his career, the Dodgers may have to pay him hundreds of millions of dollars.

Fans hold out baseballs for Bellinger to autograph.

Bellinger bats for the Glendale Desert Dogs, a minor league team, in 2016.

After high school, Bellinger spent more than four years in the minor leagues. In 2013 and 2014, he played 98 games and hit just four home runs. Then, in 2015, his power came alive. In 128 games, he thumped 30 homers.

Bellinger swings for his first MLB hit on April 25, 2017.

Bellinger got off to a hot start in the minors in 2017. The Dodgers called him up to the major leagues. On April 25, he played his first game for Los Angeles against the San Francisco Giants.

Bellinger came up to bat in the ninth inning against the Giants. He took a mighty swing, but he barely made contact with the ball. He raced to first base as the ball bounced slowly. Safe! Bellinger's first MLB hit didn't even make it to the outfield. "It's not how I imagined it would be but I'll take it," he said.

Bellinger smashes a home run against the Houston Astros in 2017.

That might have been Bellinger's shortest hit of the season. He blasted 39 home runs and won the 2017 NL Rookie of the Year award. In the World Series, the Dodgers faced the Houston Astros. Bellinger homered and had five RBIs, but Houston won in seven games.

Bellinger's 39 home runs in 2017 set a new NL record for rookies. Two years later, the record fell to Pete Alonso of the New York Mets. Alonso finished the season with 53 homers.

The Dodgers returned to the World Series in 2018 to take on the Red Sox. But like most of his teammates, Bellinger didn't hit well. Los Angeles fell in five games.

In 2019, Bellinger was the best player on his team. Then he won the NL MVP award, crowning him the best player in the league. He loves the feeling of success on the field. "So I gotta keep working really hard at what I do and hopefully, keep getting better," he said.

All-Star Stats

The Dodgers started out in Brooklyn, New York, before moving to California in 1957. They're one of MLB's oldest and most successful teams. Bellinger's career is just getting started, but he's on track to become one of the team's greatest players. Take a look at where he ranks in the top 10 on the team's single-season home run list.

Player	Home runs	Season
1. Shawn Green	49	2001
2. Adrian Beltre	48	2004
3. Cody Bellinger	47	2019
4. Sheffield	43	2000
5. Duke Snider	43	1956
6. Shawn Green	42	2002
7. Duke Snider	42	1955
8. Gil Hodges	42	1954
9. Duke Snider	42	1953
10. Roy Campanella	41	1953

Glossary

barbell: a bar with heavy disks on each end that is used for exercise

batting average: the ratio of a batter's hits per times at bat

crepe: a thin pancake

draft: when teams take turns selecting new players

minor leagues: baseball leagues where players train and prepare for MLB

off-season: the part of a year when a sports league is inactive

RBI: a run that is driven in by a batter

rookie: a first-year player

squat: an exercise performed by bending the knees and then rising

Source Notes

7 "Dodgers Beat Brewers in Game 7, Face Red Sox in World Series," ESPN, October 20, 2018, https://www.espn.com/mlb/recap?gameId=381020108.

14 Douglas Charles, "Dodgers Superstar Cody Bellinger Shared How His Workout and Diet Plan Helped Him Break Records," BroBible, accessed June 17, 2020, https://brobible.com/fitness/article/cody-bellinger-workout-diet-plans/.

17 Travis Sawchik, "Cody Bellinger Was Already Good. Then He Changed His Swing," FiveThirtyEight, May 30, 2019, https://fivethirtyeight.com/features/cody-bellinger-was-already-good-then-he-changed-his-swing/.

18–19 Richard Obert, "Cody Bellinger's Torrid Start with the Dodgers Has Hamilton Baseball Noticing," *azcentral*, April 10, 2019, https://www.azcentral.com/story/sports/high-school/2019/04/10/cody-bellingers-big-start-dodgers-has-hamilton-noticing/3427872002/.

25 Associated Press, "Clayton Kershaw Strikes Out Seven, Dodgers Beat Giants 2–1," ESPN, April 26, 2017, https://www.espn.com/mlb/recap?gameId=370425126.

27 Ken Gurnick and Sarah Wexler, "Bellinger Completes Awards Trifecta with MVP," MLB, November 19, 2019, https://www.mlb.com/news/cody-bellinger-2019-nl-mvp-award.

Learn More

Fishman, Jon M. *Baseball's G.O.A.T.: Babe Ruth, Mike Trout, and More*. Minneapolis: Lerner Publications, 2020.

Los Angeles Dodgers Foundation
https://www.mlb.com/dodgers/community/foundation

MLB
https://www.mlb.com

Official Los Angeles Dodgers Website
https://www.mlb.com/dodgers

Rhodes, Sam. *Los Angeles Dodgers*. New York: AV2 by Weigl, 2018.

Seidel, Jeff. *Pro Baseball Upsets*. Minneapolis: Lerner Publications, 2020.

Index

Photo Acknowledgments

Image credits: AP Photo/Jeff Roberson, pp. 4–5; AP Photo/Charlie Riedel, pp. 6, 7; AP Photo/Ron Frehm, p. 8; AP Photo/Carolyn Kaster, pp. 9, 11; AP Photo/Tom E. Puskar, p. 10; AP Photo/Larry Goren, p. 12; AP Photo/Will Navarro/Icon Sportswire, p. 13; AP Photo/Mark J. Terrill, pp. 14, 16; AP Photo/Tony Quinn/Icon Sportswire, p. 15; AP Photo/Brian Rothmuller, p. 18; AP Photo/Chris Pizzello, p. 20; RoidRanger/ Shutterstock.com, p. 21; AP Photo/Alex Gallardo, p. 22; AP Photo/Stephen Brashear, p. 23; AP Photo/Mike Janes, p. 24; AP Photo/Marcio Jose Sanchez, p. 25; AP Photo/ Eric Gay, p. 26.

Cover: Norm Hall/Getty Images.

Air Power

MQ-9 REAPER DRONE

LUKE COLINS

BLACK RABBIT BOOKS

Bolt is published by Black Rabbit Books
P.O. Box 3263, Mankato, Minnesota, 56002.
www.blackrabbitbooks.com

Jennifer Besel & Marysa Storm, editors;
Grant Gould, designer; Omay Ayres,
photo researcher

Library of Congress Cataloging-in-Publication Data
Names: Colins, Luke, author.
Title: MQ-9 Reaper Drone / by Luke Colins.
Description: Mankato, Minnesota : Black Rabbit Books, 2020. | Series: Bolt. Air Power | Includes bibliographical references and index. | Audience: Ages 8-12. | Audience: Grades 4 to 6.
Identifiers: LCCN 2018035505 (print) | LCCN 2018036922 (ebook) | ISBN 9781680727968 (ebook) | ISBN 9781680727906 (library binding) | ISBN 9781644660133 (paperback)
Subjects: LCSH: Reaper (Drone aircraft)—Juvenile literature.
Classification: LCC UG1242.D7 (ebook) | LCC UG1242.D7 C65 2020 (print) | DDC 623.74/69—dc23
LC record available at https://lccn.loc.gov/2018035505

Printed in the United States. 1/19

Image Credits

aerofly-sim.de: Aerofly, Cover (drone); af.mil: 1st Lt. Shannon Collins / US Air Force, 1; Airman 1st Class Michael Shoemaker/US Air Force, 3, 18–19; Lt. Col. Leslie Pratt/US Air Force, 4–5, 26–27; Samuel King Jr./US Air Force, 11 (r); af.mil, US Air Force, 9 (b), 13 (bl & tr), 31; afcent.af.mil, Staff Sgt. Brian Ferguson/US Air Force, 10 (b); commons.wikimedia.org: Brigadier Lance Mans / NATO Special Operations Coordination Centre, 13 (tl); US Air Force, 10 (t); commons.wikimedia.org/af.mil: Master Sergeant Steve Horton/US Air Force, 26 (tr); commons.wikimedia.org/defenceimagery.mod.uk: Cpl Mark Webster, 15 (t); commons.wikimedia.org/usda.gov: U.S. Department of Agriculture, 25 (bkgd); defenceupdate.in: Indian Defence Update, 28–29; digitalcombatsimulator.com: topergood, 6–7 (drone), 27 (b); eglin.af.mil: US Air Force, 11 (l); en.wikipedia.org/af.mil: Paul Ridgeway/US Air Force, 20–21; fas.org: US Air Force, 12 (t); Getty: Ethan Miller, 15 (b); gtaall.com: SkylineGTRFreak, 25 (drone); i-hls.com: iHLS, 22; nationalmuseum.af.mil: US Air Force, 12 (b); Shutterstock: boscorelli, 9 (t); Genova, Cover (clouds); Getmilitaryphotos, 6–7 (bkgd); Handatko, 26 (tl); inspired-fiona, 16 (bkgd); Michael Fitzsimmons, 32; simpleplanes.com: BobTheTitanSP, 12–13 (bkgd); twitter.com: RamiAILoIah, 13 (br); ssl-forum.com: US Air Force, 16–17

CONTENTS

CHAPTER 1

Taking Out the ENEMY

The MQ-9 Reaper **drone** zoomed down the runway. It lifted into the air. Then it soared toward its target. The drone was on a mission. **Terrorists** in Afghanistan were selling drugs. The drone was going to destroy their buildings.

Mission Accomplished

The Reaper flew about 100 miles (161 kilometers). When it got to the target, its cameras recorded the area. Then it dropped four 500-pound (227-kilogram) bombs. The buildings exploded. Then the drone flew away.

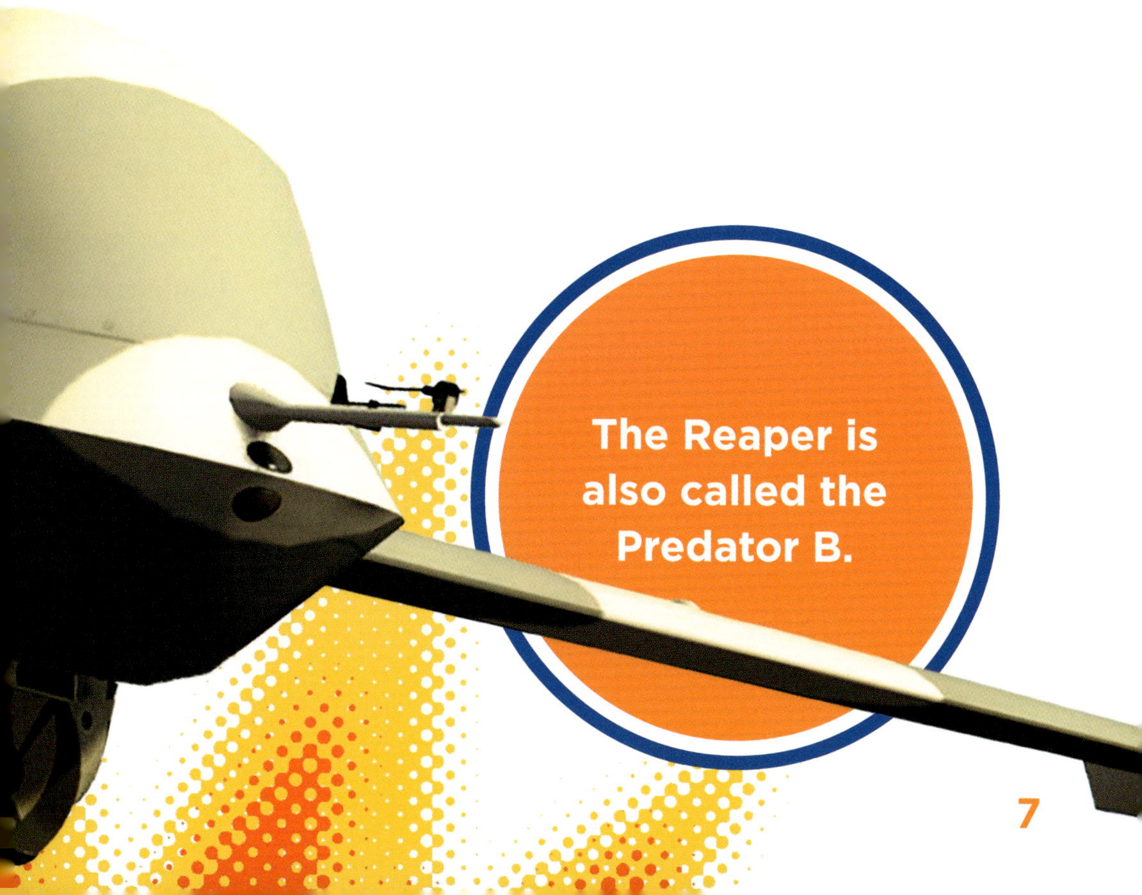

The Reaper is also called the Predator B.

CHAPTER 2

HISTORY of the MQ-9 Reaper Drone

The Reaper's history starts in the 1990s. The U.S. military began using Predator drones. At first, the drones didn't carry weapons. They were used to find targets. But eventually, the military put weapons on them.

MQ-1B Predator vs. MQ-9 Reaper

MQ-1B Predator		MQ-9 Reaper
2,250 pounds (1,021 kg)	maximum takeoff weight	10,500 pounds (4,763 kg)
up to 770 miles (1,239 km)	range	up to 1,150 miles (1,851 km)
55 feet (17 meters)	wingspan	79 feet (24 m)

Weapons the Reaper Carries

GBU-38
precision bomb

Improving the Drones

Engineers worked to improve **remotely** piloted aircraft (RPA). In 2005, the U.S. Air Force ordered a new drone. This drone would carry more weapons. It could also go faster and farther. They called it the MQ-9 Reaper.

GBU-12 Paveway II
laser-guided bomb

AGM-114
Hellfire missile

REAPER DRONE TIMELINE

1995

The first Predator RQ-1 is used for missions.

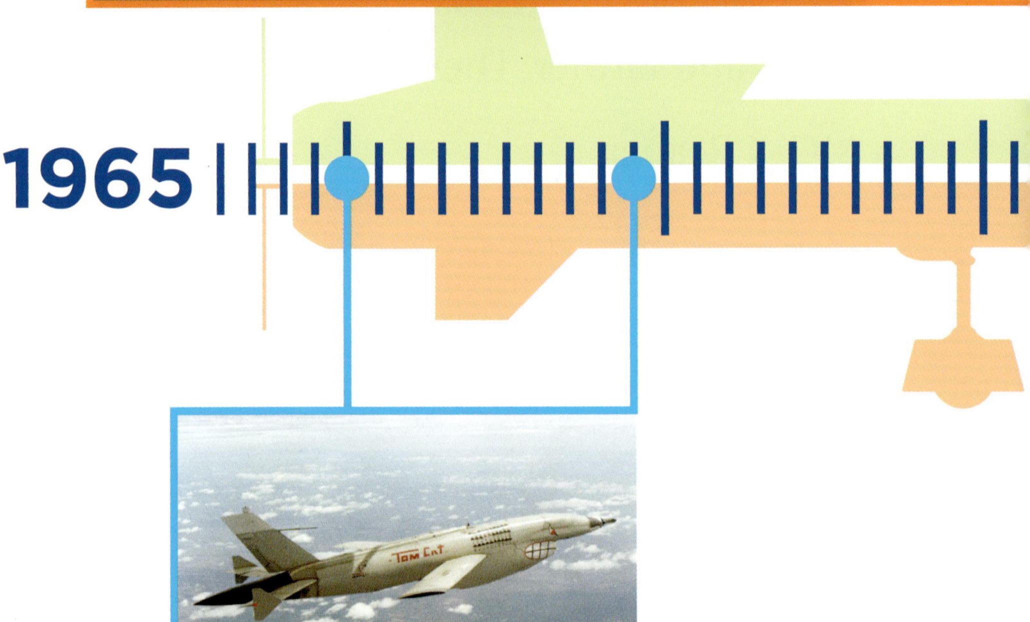

1970s

The U.S. military uses RPAs in **combat**.

October

2001

A Predator carries out the first successful drone strike.

March

2005

The U.S. Air Force orders MQ-9 Reapers.

2020

October

2007

Reapers enter combat.

February

2018

A Reaper bombs buildings in Afghanistan.

CHAPTER 3

Reaper Drone FEATURES

One of the Reaper's jobs is to gather information. The drone has one or two pods **mounted** on it. The pods carry up to 368 cameras. Soldiers use the cameras' images to decide where to strike.

The drones can record at night. They use lasers to light up an area.

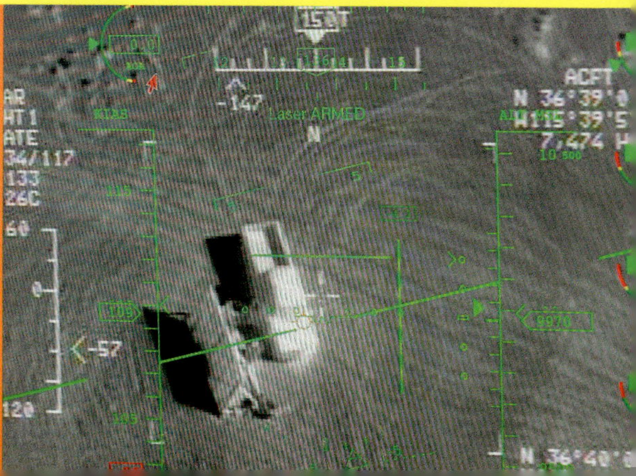

REAPER DRONE STATS

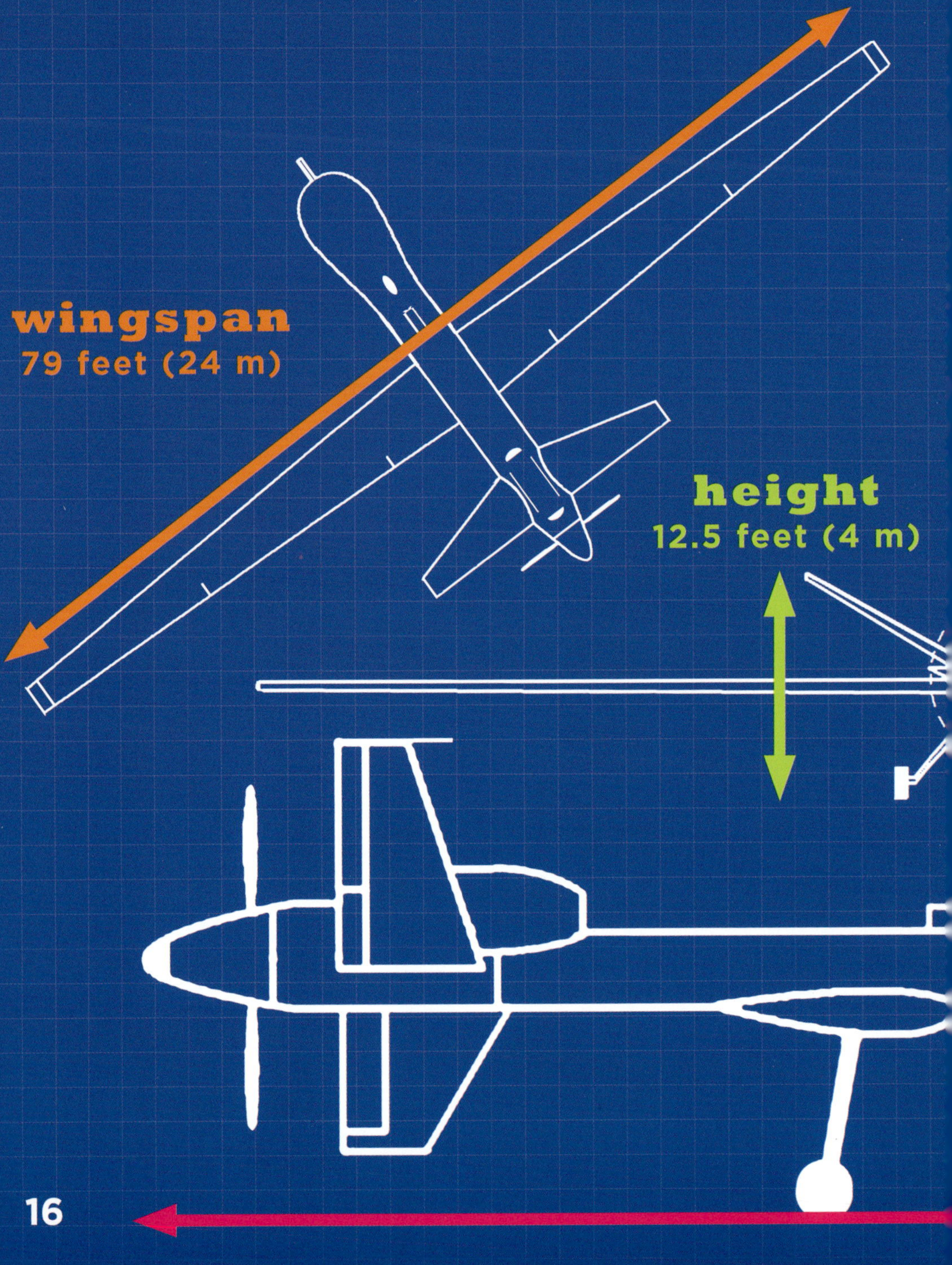

On Target

The Reaper carries some big weapons. But it needs to know where to drop them. The drone has a laser range finder. This equipment guides bombs to an exact spot.

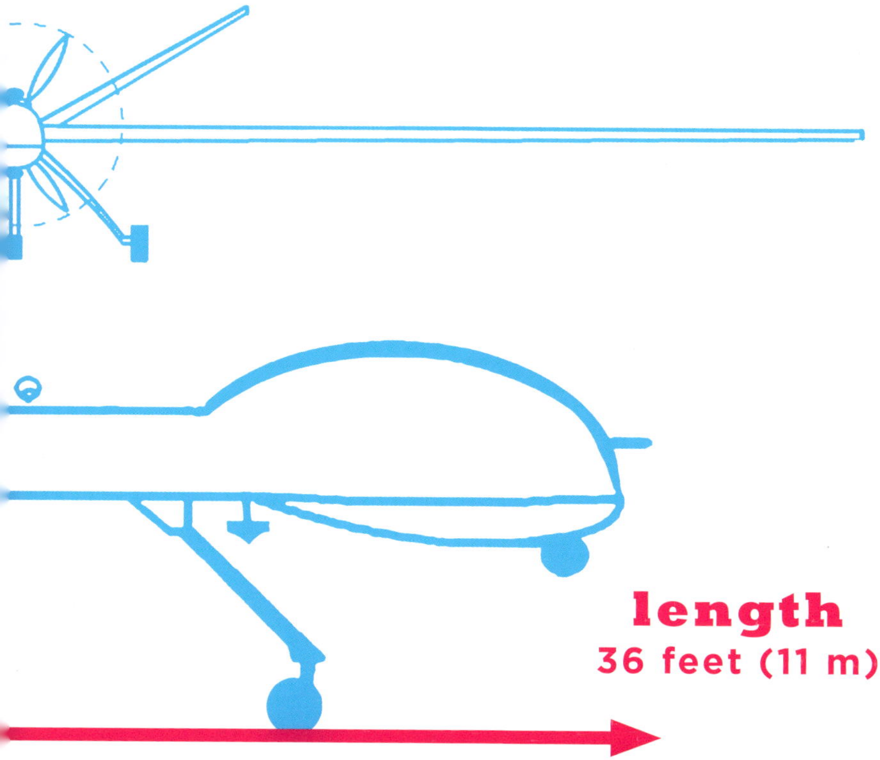

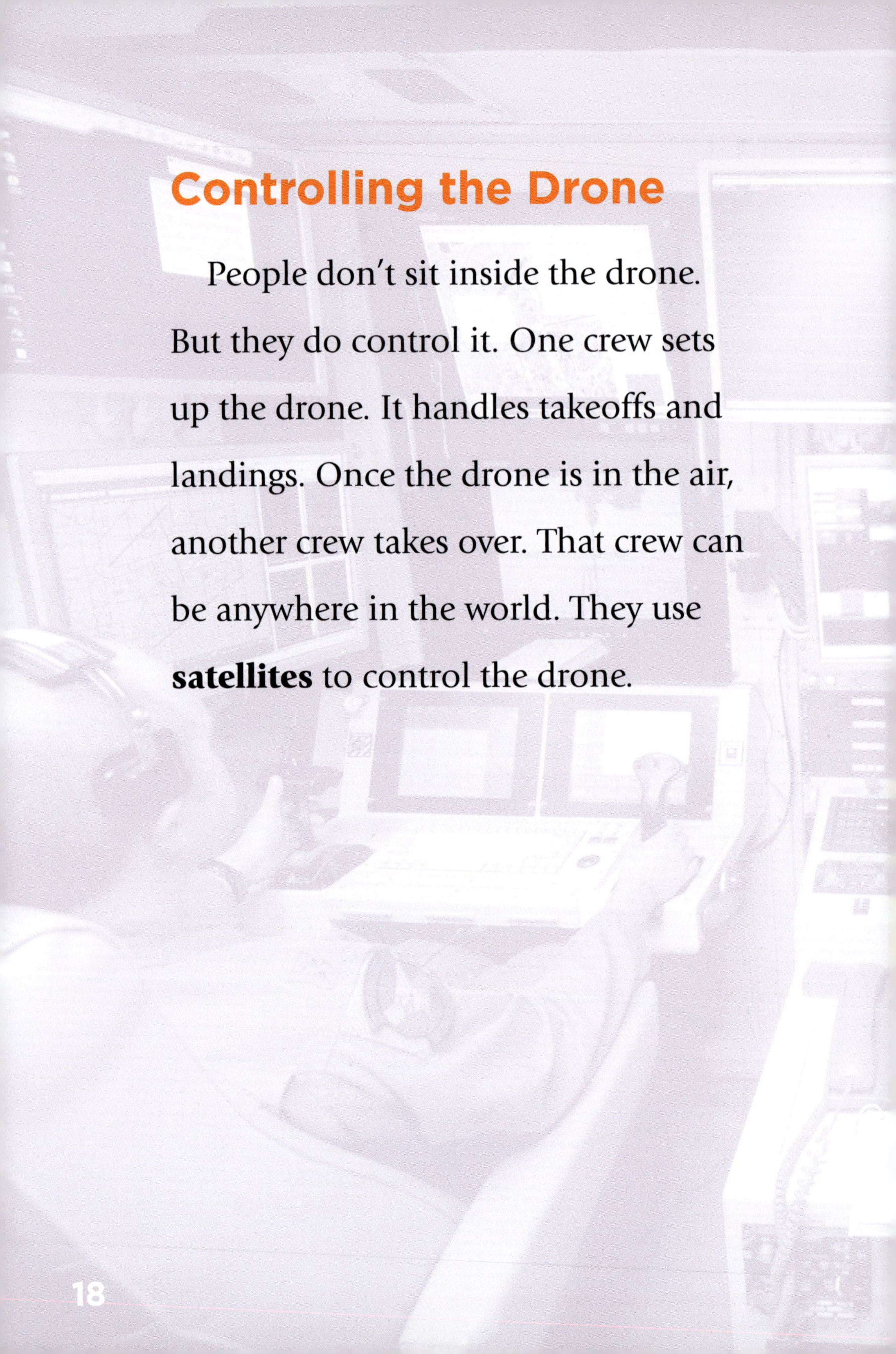

Controlling the Drone

People don't sit inside the drone. But they do control it. One crew sets up the drone. It handles takeoffs and landings. Once the drone is in the air, another crew takes over. That crew can be anywhere in the world. They use **satellites** to control the drone.

TUTOR ET ULTOR

REAPER DRONE PARTS

PAYLOAD BAY
CAMERAS AND SENSORS

CHAPTER 4

The Reaper Drone in ACTION

Reapers are used all around the world. In 2017, U.S. forces used them to gather information in Yemen. In 2018, U.S. Reapers flew from Poland. No one is saying what their mission was.

Countries that Use Reapers

France
Italy
United Kingdom
United States

Helping Out

Reapers aren't just useful during war. In 2017, Reapers flew over wildfires in California. They took pictures of the fires. Firefighters used the photos to see where fires were spreading.

BY THE NUMBERS

4,000 pounds

(1,814 kg)

HOW MUCH FUEL IT CAN CARRY

2

CREW NEEDED TO PILOT THE CRAFT

276 miles
(444 km) per hour

TOP SPEED

50,000 FEET
(15,240 m)
how high the drone can fly

A Powerful Tool and Weapon

Reapers are powerful tools. They carry big weapons. And they go into dangerous areas. These drones will help people well into the future.

GLOSSARY

combat (kahm-BAT)—active fighting, often in a war

drone (DROHN)—an unmanned aircraft or ship guided by remote control or onboard computer

engineer (en-juh-NEER)—a designer or builder

mount (MOUNT)—to attach

payload (PAY-lohd)—the load carried by a vehicle necessary to the purpose of its job

remotely (ree-MOHT-lee)—distant or far away

satellite (SA-tuh-liyt)—a machine sent into space that moves around the earth, moon, sun, or other planet

sensor (SEN-sor)—a device that finds heat, light, sound, motion, or other things

terrorist (TER-ur-ist)—a person who uses violent acts to frighten people in order to achieve a goal

LEARN MORE

BOOKS

Gray, Judy Silverstein, and Taylor Baldwin Kiland. *Drones: Remote-Controlled Warfare*. Military Engineering in Action. New York: Enslow Publishing, 2016.

Lanier, Wendy Hinote. *Drones*. Let's Fly. Lake Elmo, MN: Focus Readers, 2019.

Larson, Kirsten W. *Drones*. Robotics in Our World. Mankato, MN: Amicus High Interest/Amicus Ink, 2018.

WEBSITES

How the MQ-9 Reaper Works
science.howstuffworks.com/reaper.htm

MQ-9 Reaper
www.af.mil/About-Us/Fact-Sheets/Display/Article/104470/mq-9-reaper/

Predator B RPA
www.ga-asi.com/predator-b

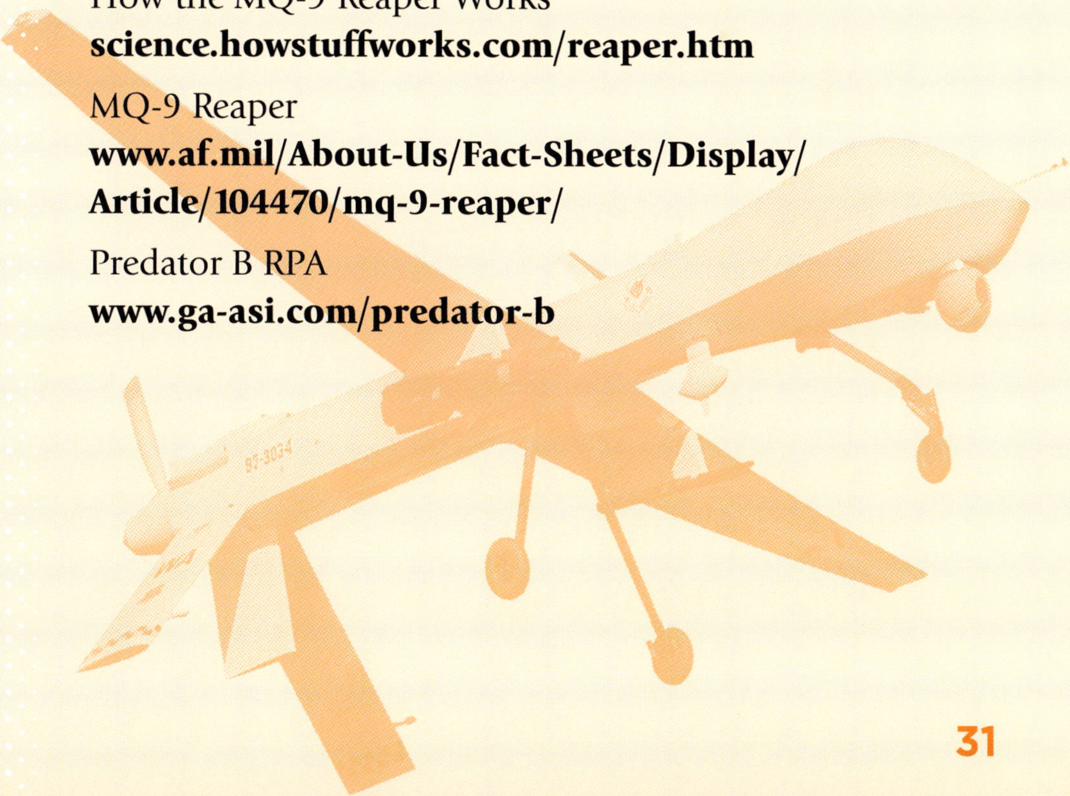

INDEX